May 19th, 2016
1st fathers day to my
soon to be father

I Love My Dad

I Love My Dad

by Caroline Bell

Fitzhenry & Whiteside

For Jim and David
and in memory of my father,
John Thelwall Evans

© Fitzhenry & Whiteside 1988

Fitzhenry & Whiteside
195 Allstate Parkway
Markham, Ontario L3R 4T8

Canadian Cataloguing in Publication Data

Bell, Caroline, 1953-
  I love my dad

ISBN 0-88902-736-6

I. Title.

PS8553.E454I14 1987   jC813'.54   C87-0953235-8
PZ7.B45I1 1987

Printed in Hong Kong

I love my Dad
because…

He likes to doze with me in the morning.

Sometimes we snack on junk food.

He has an outfit just like mine.

He likes to play with me.

We dig the same kind of music.

He takes an interest in what I'm doing.

He fixes the broken parts.

He always lends a helping hand.

We work well together.

He can bring me out of my shell.

He answers all my questions.

He's my best friend.

He's someone I look up to.

I feel safe when he's near.

He always wants a bedtime hug.

He teaches me to be me.

But best of all, I brighten his day,
because I'm his son.

Printed and bound in Hong Kong